THE TYCOON'S

Replacement Bride (2)

[Billionaire Romance: BBW]

MONTANA NIGHT

WARNING this erotic romance novelette contains explicit language and graphic sexual content. If you are under the age of eighteen or are sensitive to erotic language please put this book down, it is not appropriate for you.

Printed in the United States

ACKNOWLEDGMENTS

To my husband, because *he is the wind beneath my wings*. To my mother because without her I would never have been. To my friends because their encouragement was invaluable. To my readers for loving my books. To you all I say thank you.

Montana Night

PREVIOUSLY (PART 1)

Amanda Cardwell's best friend Emma Baker arranged to be a mail-order bride for Billionaire Tycoon Grant Hamilton. But she backs out last minute, so her friend Amanda steps in to save the day. After all, one look at her curvy self and the billionaire will cancel the marriage contract and that will be that. At least that was the plan.

But she didn't count on the sex-factor. A fake replacement mail-order bride mix-up turns into a very real engagement, with a real man. But the path of love is never a smooth one, and Amanda is just about to learn how true that is.

CHAPTER 1

Amanda Cardwell woke up in a brightly lit room that looked taken straight out of *Arabian Nights*. A lock of auburn hair tumbled across her face; she hurriedly hooked it behind her throbbing ear with shaky hands. She stumbled out of the four-poster bed and made her way over to a big bay window to the opposite side of the room. Looking out of the window, her mouth dropped open. *Oh my gosh!*

For miles in all directions the only thing Amanda could see was sand.

She started racking her foggy brain for an explanation. *How did I get here?* Her brain stubbornly refused to give her an answer. *Think Amanda!*

Dread started spreading its clammy tenterhooks through her veins. However hard she tried her brain was not about to co-operate. She couldn't remember a thing. *Calm down.*

Taking a couple of deep breaths she realized it wasn't true. She did remember some things. She knew that adding two and two would get you four, that the sun always rose in the east, and that the Chicago Cubs were never going to win the World Series again. And she knew her own name. Well, the first one at least. She had no idea what her last name was, how she'd ended up in this room, or why she could smell rosemary and myrrh incense so thickly in the air.

Scared with all that wasn't rushing back to her, Amanda surged to her feet. Frantically she looked around. She spotted a beautiful ornate door and decided it was better to find somewhere to hide quickly and *then* try to figure out what had happened to her. As she tiptoed through the door she stopped right in her track. A sliver of panic ran down her spine.

Her surroundings looked like she'd fallen onto the set of *Arabian Nights.* The women staring back at her---and there had to be almost four dozen---were gorgeous. Thin but with heaving bosoms, skin bronzed from the sun and from their natural complexion, and the flattest midriffs she'd ever seen. Amanda noted that she was dressed in a long black flowing robe, like she remembered seeing in a lot of Middle Eastern women, minus the head coverings. Meanwhile, everyone else was decked out in flowing pants that made her think of genies.

With almost fifty exotic beauties surrounding her, bedecked in bangles and the finest silks, she felt like the odd duckling. Tentatively she ran her hands down her body. Relieved, she noted that she had been blessed with an hourglass shaped figure. But it was clear that she was *oh so* far from supermodel size. *Can't complain about the boobs or the junk in the trunk though.*

Arching her neck around, she groaned again at the way her pants fit too snugly. Something else flicked through her memory and Amanda threw off the black garment covering her. Underneath, she still wore plain jeans and a white T-shirt. *Clearly I am not part of this harem. So what am I doing here?*

A few of the women were edging towards her and Amanda stumbled backwards. She turned around and ran over the collection of thick red and gold rugs, woven with the most intricate of patterns, and desperately looked for another way out of the immense room. The windows were covered in thick bars made of iron, at the sight her heart almost stopped. Wherever she was, she wasn't leaving any time soon, maybe not ever again. *Perfect.*

She didn't know who she was, and she didn't know where she was except a desert. Tears welled up in her eyes and she slid down the wall and to the floor.

The sea of inhumanly gorgeous women parted from in front of her. An elderly matron, rotund and shapeless under her coverings, knelt down before her. On either side of the woman stood guards. Their necks were the size of tree trunks, and they carried both scimitars on their left hips and nine mils in a holster over their right shoulders.

Nope. She was never leaving. *I've really done it this time.*

That was the last thought to cross her mind before darkness overtook her. But reality came quickly crashing back through smelling salts from hell. The stench could only be described as ten times worse than sewers. *Right, clearly fainting isn't the answer. I'm still here.*

As hard as she was trying to go back to blissful unconsciousness the women surrounding her didn't seem to want to let her. The army of beauties was babbling away in

Arabic. So they were making zero sense to Amanda. The only discernible words were *Mr. Assad* and *doctor.* As the guards motioned with their scimitars towards the door, Amanda assumed they wanted to take her to some kind of examination. By now, her head was throbbing, and she was fervently hoping this examination was going to be external only.

***

DR. ASSAD TURNED OUT to be a kindly little man with lines at the corner of his eyes and a long graying beard that tickled Amanda's arms as he leaned in to take her temperature.

"Ms. Cardwell, how are you feeling today?" Dr. Assad prodded as he listened to her chest. Idly, Amanda wondered if he could feel it race as badly as she did.

"Wretched. Confused. I can't remember who I am. I…well. I don't know what to think. How did I get here?" A terrifying thought, straight from the cheesiest movies she had ever seen, flashed through her mind. "Am I here to be some dirty old sheikh's whore?" Amanda blurted, blushed, and then clamped her mouth shut. *Please, please tell me I'm wrong.*

The doctor smiled back at her, making his eyes twinkle just a bit, almost like Santa. "I am just an old man, Ms. Cardwell, but I understand. I think you've gotten quite the wrong impression of Master Alid."

"Master Alid?"

"Yes, Sheikh Samir Ben Alid, he is the Master of this harem. I've known Samir since he was a child. I was first his father's personal physician."

"Oh, I'm sorry."

Dr. Assad smiled indulgently as he pulled out a pen light to inspect her eyes; she blinked at the onslaught. "His father is very much alive as are his three brothers. He is a young man by my standards. When he moved to Oman, I chose to go with him. He's a good man, works hard to make sure his family's company gives to worthy charities, and the way he is with Jasmine--"

It suddenly felt cold in the room. "Is she also in the harem?"

"His little sister, but you'll meet more people here soon enough," he finished, going over to his counter. "Ms. Cardwell, you don't appear to have anything wrong with you apart from your concussion."

She rubbed her head as if a knot would magically appear there. "I don't doubt I had a concussion. This amnesia must have come from somewhere. I can't recall family or friends. My life before waking up here is shrouded in darkness. It is like someone has erased part of my past. "

"A serious blow to the head like you had can lead to retrograde amnesia. Retrograde amnesia means you have lost memories for events PRIOR to the head injury accident. For some people, the amnesia can cover just a minute or even a few seconds. For other people, like in your case, amnesia may affect longer periods of time.

"What does this mean? Am I ever going to get my memory back?"

"As people get better from their head injuries, long-term memories tend to return. If you are lucky, your memory will be triggered by smell, sound, or something visual and you will be yourself again."

"And if I am unlucky?"

"Then your memories will return like fragments of a jigsaw puzzle; bits and pieces returning in random order."

Amanda sat in silence for several minutes as the doctor continued his examination. Every nerve ending of her body was screaming at her to run. Taking a deep breath, she willed her heart to stop thudding in her chest. What she needed now were facts. "How did I get here if I wasn't taken?"

"Of course, in the Middle East we are all in the business of stealing Western women," the doctor replied harshly, the insult clear in his voice.

Amanda blushed and looked away, realizing how terrible her accusations sounded when said aloud. "I apologize. I didn't mean it that way, to play on stereotypes. Still, I wake up behind bars literally so what am I supposed to think?"

"Your family accrued substantial gambling debts as I've heard it. Master Alid paid them and sent your father to gambling rehabilitation. You agreed to come live as part of the harem for two years as part of the compensation. He offered other methods, but you were quite insistent."

"I was?" Amanda exclaimed, her brow creased in confusion.

"Assuredly from what I heard. He saved your family and you wanted to come be a part of his life here from gratitude. Whatever you might think…Master Alid is a great man."

Amanda sighed and was grateful when Dr. Assad left to allow her some time to reconcile with what she had just been told. One single thought lingered in her mind.

She did this to herself.

CHAPTER 2

The hot summer sun blazed down on Billionaire Tycoon Grant Hamilton as he got out of the Learjet in Tel Aviv. He wasn't that fond of the Middle East. While there were certain elements of the culture, and especially in his younger years, the women that he enjoyed, the constant sun and heat wore at him. It wasn't like Florida either, where the heat was interspersed with rain, clouds, or pleasant breezes that came off the ocean at night. Here in the Middle East, it was sandblasting furnace hot, almost constantly.

"*Barukh ha-ba* Mr. Hamilton. I trust your flight was comfortable?" an older Israeli man greeted him. His name was Levi, with no last name. He was a retired Mossad agent who now worked in the private sector. Both Grant's younger brothers Alexander and Chase had endorsed his skills.

After pouring over the records of the Harbormaster in Florida, Grant had called on Chase, who used his private contacts to trace the ship to the Middle East. From there though, Chase was lost, as his security company CorpSec focused mainly in the Americas and East Asia. Alexander had offered to step in and help, but he was currently handling an assignment for the CIA. It left Grant by himself, although both brothers swore to drop everything and come if needed. Their last piece of assistance was Levi's name and contact information.

"*Shalom* Master Levi, I appreciate your hospitality. The journey was as tolerable as possible under the circumstances. As this is a matter of urgency let's move straight to business. What have your sources discovered?"

"We have traced her to Oman, but more than that I cannot say for sure. We know the specific men who took your fiancée, but so far we have not been able to track down their whereabouts. Do you have any idea who might have wanted to kidnap your fiancée beyond this Natasha that your staff mentioned?"

"No," Grant replied in a terse voice. "My business dealings have been world-wide, and not all of those deals have ended with all parties happy. However I can't imagine any of my competitors or ex-business partners doing anything like this." He could not disguise the strained tone of his voice.

"I have experience in such matters, Mr. Hamilton," Levi continued, leading him towards a small building off to the side of the main terminal. "My associates are doing their best to find the exact location of the girl's kidnappers as we speak."

"Amanda," Grant hissed, his anger surprising them both. "She's not 'the girl,' she's not just my fiancée. She is a person and her name is Amanda."

Levi nodded, sympathy clouding his features. "Of course. Amanda. If I may give some professional advice?"

Grant took a deep breath. He knew he was being unreasonable and difficult with people who didn't have to help him. But guilt gnawed his innards like a rabid dog. *I should have protected her.*

Not answering until Levi had pulled open the door and led him inside, he sighed in appreciation of the air conditioning. "Go ahead, Levi. Please accept my apologies for becoming so heated."

"Apology accepted. Emotions are not a bad thing, Mr. Hamilton. My people have learned that without the passions of your heart, your enemies will eventually win. But, you cannot let your passion's flame so fiercely as to consume you both. Then you will definitely lose."

Grant nodded, his resolve reconfirmed. "Wise words, Levi. No wonder my brothers like you."

"Mr. Chase only has an affinity for me because he and my son share similar bad tastes in music," Levi said with a smile, leading Grant towards his company's operations center. Inside, Grant saw three other people, two stunningly beautiful Israeli women and a man who Grant thought may have been an Arab of some sort.

Levi made introductions. "Mr. Hamilton, let me introduce my intelligence staff. The two ladies you see are Talia and Roni Ben-David, twin sisters. They are computer hackers whose skill is only surpassed by their matchless beauty. The handsome gentleman with them Rashn, who like me prefers to go by only one name."

"Thank you all for your assistance," Grant replied, the cultured tones and niceties of society falling into place with unconscious ease. He may not have liked the Middle East for the weather, but he hadn't completed all the deals he had without at least some manners. "You have my gratitude."

"Levi, Talia was able to crack into the accounts you asked about," the woman Grant assumed was Roni said immediately. "We were able to track two separate emails, one to a bar in Abu Dhabi, another to a so far anonymous account in Oman itself. We have names on the kidnappers you requested."

"Do you have their current whereabouts?" Levi asked, a sanguine smile spreading over his face. *Soto voce*, he whispered to Grant. "See? I told you they were good."

"Yes," Talia replied, taking over for her sister. "The sender of the email is on his way to Riyadh at this time."

Grant nodded, and looked over at Rashn. "Do you have any additional information to report?"

The man shook his head, crossing his arms over his chest.

"All right then. Levi, my jet can be refueled and ready to fly in an hour. It looks like we're heading to Riyadh." *I'm coming for you, just hold one. Be safe.*

Levi nodded, a grin breaking out wider on his face. "It's been a while. I wonder if the Saudis still remember me?"

CHAPTER 3

As Amanda was walked back to the main harem compound, she found herself surrounded again. Out of the sea of concubines an older woman stepped forward, reached out, and stroked her hair. Amanda took a step backwards.

"Who are you people?" she demanded, hating how her voice wouldn't come out as more than a whimper. "Do you live in this harem?"

A woman sashayed out from behind the taller of the two guards. Her hips swayed with seductive authority; she oozed sensuality and knew it. Hazel eyes heavy with mascara bore into her own eyes and Amanda gulped. Why did she find her even scarier than the guards with weapons? She stopped, looking as if she had swallowed something exceedingly bitter.

"I am Nadia, supreme mistress of this estate. Our master, the honorable Sheikh Samir Ben-Alid, has ordered us to welcome you to his harem." Having taken a moment to regain her composure, she straightened up swaying her hips, the bangles adorning their slim dimensions jangling for all to hear.

"I find you lacking, American, but the master wishes as he wishes, and his wish is our command."

"Really?" Amanda remarked; pleased at how nonchalant she sounded. She wasn't skinny with fitness model abdominals like Nadia was, but she wasn't going to put up with anyone's stinky attitude either. Whoever she had been, Amanda already knew she was a fighter. She was determined not to reveal to these people exactly how scared she was. Taking a deep breath she added with a smile of defiance, "I don't particularly want to meet him. Maybe another day."

"Foolish girl. It is an honor." Nadia said with disdain. "What you wish stopped mattering the moment you agreed to be here," she continued more calmly, her voice containing an underlying hint of ice.

"So I've been told. I still don't believe I am the kind of person who would want to be locked up in a harem. Seriously, why would I?"

"Because you are a *sharmuta*, a whore who needed rescuing," Nadia snapped. She eyed the older woman standing at her right, her voice calming as she issued her commands. "The bath oils first.... and then find this *bin'nt himaar* something that might hope to fit her."

The older woman nodded, but struggled to bend down to pull off Amanda's T-shirt. Nadia's next command—whatever it was ---was in Arabic, but it was motivating enough for the older woman and several of the other girls to strip Amanda to her underwear. They didn't stop there however, as two of the younger girls started to pull down her panties, while another two held her arms and the third unclasped her bra. Her heavy breasts spilled out like cream topped with a cherry, bouncing delicately at their sudden freedom. Amanda had never felt so humiliated and helpless in her life. An unwelcome blush crept into her cheeks.

Despite the situation, it was Nadia's hot stare, trailing leisurely from her round breasts to the auburn patch between her legs, that made her most uncomfortable.

"Our master likes a shaven *koos*, so your lovely bush will unfortunately have to go." Nadia walked up to her and started caressing her neck leisurely. Amanda thought she was going to melt from the embarrassment. The entire harem was watching in silence. What kind of crazy rabbit hole had she fallen into?

"I..." she stammered her flush deepening to crimson. "Stop it!"

Spying her discomfort, Nadia replied icily. "Master Alid will soon grow tired of you, but no need to worry."

Nadia grinned, but Amanda had seen sharks with friendlier expressions on the Discovery Channel. "When you're found wanting, *sharmuta*, I will get to give you my special brand of attention."

From the look in her eyes, Amanda knew it wasn't punishment Nadia was aiming for. *I need to get the heck out of here.*

***

AFTER WHAT SEEMED like an eternity Amanda found herself oiled, powdered, and getting a manicure from an older woman in the harem. Behind her, two girls took turns with her hair. After shampooing it, they rubbed luxurious conditioners in, rinsing it multiple times before applying scented oils. They tried braiding it in a pair of ropes down her back, but the older of the two girls, whose jet black hair glistened in the steamy heat of the bath and hung straight down the middle of her back, with a beautiful tiger's eye amulet at her copper colored throat, had hated it. After an exchange of heated, foreign words, the younger girl with hair more magenta than red, had pulled everything down. Now they were back to the drawing board. This time, they used curling irons to help pile Amanda's long locks up in an up-do with tendrils raining from it. The older woman had found flower petals and jeweled hair combs to accent everything. She had no living memory of ever looking this beautiful. While she wanted to go home, wherever that was, somehow she couldn't stop herself from wanting to be as beautiful as the women around her were. *No longer the ugly duckling?* she thought, as they showed her the results in a hand mirror. The style was flattering and would please this Master Alid, according to the old woman. Even Amanda could only agree. Odd that she should be concerned by what a mystery sheikh thought of her.

Even though her worst fears had ebbed after her third hour of pampering, she was very aware a man now had the right to do whatever he wanted with her body. *Take a deep breath. You can get through this.*

The tranquil location of the harem, with richly adorned facilities, soft silken clothing, and gilded accents was oddly soothing. So far, it seemed as long as she didn't stare too hard at the guards by the door, Amanda could almost forget she was now property. After Nadia's threats, she had expected to be flogged and set out in some palace square in stocks. Shouldn't Alid that pervert sultan or whatever he was, have burst in here by now to have his way with her? Amanda gulped. *Reality check – Yep. I am still freaked out.*

Nervously, she looked back to the poor magenta-haired girl and was quickly urged to set her head back into place. "I'm sorry. I just…not that I want Nadia to come back, but I thought this would be worse. Was I wrong?"

The oldest woman chuckled. "Nadia speaks angrily, but she was his favorite before. She would dance and Master Alid would fall down at her feet. For years she had been his favorite, but since your arrival, she has found herself in an unfamiliar position."

"It seems," the raven haired woman added, "That this change has caused her personality to come through in new ways, though. Nadia was always a terror. She has very unique tastes and…never mind. Let's just say that I'm glad someone got bumped off the pedestal. She's a – what do you Americans call it – a bitch?"

Amanda burst out laughing "Yes, I guess a bitch is exactly what she is." Both women started laughing uncontrollably. The girl leaned over and bowed her head a bit toward Amanda. "I'm Dyana, by the way. I've been here for a long time, maybe five years. It's not as bad as you think. We've all come of our own free will, often as favors for our families. We're cared for and

Master Alid...." Dyana's voice trailed off, as a blush rose to her cheeks.

The magenta-hair girl laughed loudly even as she added the first pins for Amanda's emerald green veil. "What my sister means is that man knows how to pleasure a woman. The worst day isn't joining the harem. It's always when he finds another one. We're still given some access, the lucky ones at least, but once you have a lover of that skill... well being trapped here isn't so bad. We're all spoiled for other men."

"Odella!" Dyana chided. "That's too much. She means that Master is very kind and, ahem, generous."

"Yes, generous enough that I'm stuck here with prison bars and armed guards. You all sound like educated, modern women. Why are you voluntarily staying here as a slave?" Amanda asked, puzzled.

"There are many reasons the women of the Sheikh stay, and many reasons why the Master has guards," the older woman said, working with surprising speed with the pale pink nail polish on Amanda's pinkie. "First, there are many who would seek to steal these girls, to keep them for their own. The guards are far more for their well-being than to keep them from fleeing."

"That all sounds very charming, if you were raised in the Middle East. I still want to go home!"

Odella tutted and finished settling the veil over Amanda's head. It fell to cover her face so that now she could only see through the eye slit. The sheer fabric was very breathable however, and she didn't feel at all stifled by the airy garment. "You don't even know where that is and, believe me Miss; you can't imagine how fortunate you are."

Amanda sighed and wasn't sure what to think. Samir had saved her family. It could be a lie, but then both Dyana and Odella said that Samir was about as amazing as it gets. Hell, Nadia wouldn't be such a jealous bitch if he wasn't worth holding onto.

Speak of the Devil, and she shall appear. Nadia sashayed into the room, heading straight for Amanda. Using just her eyes and a sharp gesture, she commanded the guards, who moved to either side of Amanda, seizing her in their immensely powerful hands.

"Time for your treatment," Nadia said with a seductively, devilish smile.

CHAPTER 4

As she lay tied down to what looked like a X shaped massage table, Amanda felt her heart racing. The humiliation of having all of her clothes stripped off of her for the second time still stung. Tied, Amanda could only stare at the ceiling, glimpsing her crotch as she lay on the table.

Nadia had sent everyone else away, decreeing she would be waxing the *sharmuta* personally before leaving her alone for what seemed like an eternity. Despite straining to release herself, the silk ties Nadia had used held her firmly in place. Exhausted from her futile attempts Amanda stilled. Out of the corner of her eye she could see beautifully ornate shelves and furniture, creams, and lotions. It then dawned on her that whatever this "treatment" was she could not stop what was about to happen. As Amanda wondered what kind of perverted game she was to be exposed to, Nadia walked back into the room. Amanda had never felt so powerless in her life.

Nadia's eyes trailed over her naked body as she walked

towards her, causing Amanda to blush. She resolved that whatever was going to happen she would survive and make Nadia pay. With trepidation she clenched her eyes closed and waited for the assault.

Nothing happened.

After what seemed like an eternity she cranked one eye open. Nadia was busily fiddling away with some vials.

"Well are you going to get on with it or what?" Amanda tried to sound defiant, but anxiety spurted through her.

"You are eager for my attention, that is good," replied Nadia. She turned around and unceremoniously started massaging Amanda with a concoction that smelt like evening primrose oil mixed with almond and something else Amanda could not identify.

It felt... marvelous. Amanda almost melted at the pleasure. She hadn't allowed herself to acknowledge how sore and battered she had felt since her awakening. Now Nadia's supple fingers soothed away all the aches, and she almost purred. Confused but determined not to waste time trying to understand the strange goings on she closed her eyes and let herself enjoy the relaxing massage. But soon she noticed something was off. The oil was creating a strange sensation wherever Nadia touched. The sensation grew with every stroke.

"Ah, I see the oil is starting to work its magic," Nadia whispered in her ear. Amanda's eyes popped open.

Nadia was standing *so very close.* Looking her deep in the eyes, she slowly started working the oil around her pubic hair. Making sure she spread her vagina lips to cover every corner. In the process she accidently stroked Amanda's clit. A delicious tendril of desire shot through her body. *How-, what the hell?!*

Confused, Amanda didn't know what to think. She didn't think she had ever let a woman touch her before. It didn't matter that her memory was gone; she thought she would remember that. Convinced it must have been a mistake, she kept her eyes glued to the harem Mistress.

With deft fingers Nadia continued her ministration by rubbing the liquid concoction over her crotch, spending extra attention on the area around her labia. Nadia's labored breath echoed through the room. With one hand still casually stroking Amanda's crotch, she reached over, smearing some sort of wax from a jar over her entire nether region. Amanda bit her lower lip, confused at what the heck was happening. Embarrassed and convinced she was just misunderstanding; she shut her mouth and closed her eyes. This was a wax and nothing else.

Just as anxiety was giving way to relaxation Nadia accidently pinched her clit trying to spread wax along her vaginal lips. Amanda couldn't help it; the sensations caused her to moan out load, before she could bite it back.

Now wary about what was next to come, Amanda tried to glimpse what Nadia was doing. With concentration the Harem Mistress was spreading the wax mixture evenly so it totally covered all of Amanda's pubic hair. She withdrew her hands momentarily to wipe them clean on a soft terrycloth towel. She then picked up a strip of muslin cloth, and spread it over some of the waxy area on the inside of Amanda's right thigh.

With one swift move Nadia pulled up the cloth, the wax uprooting Amanda's pubic hair, leaving behind a one inch wide strip of smooth, bare skin. Amanda almost bucked off the table.

The pain was intense. But what followed, an aftermath of pure desire was what left her gasping. *How is this possible?*

She intuitively knew that she wasn't the type of girl to enjoy casual sex. Despite her denial, she could feel wetness start to seep from her pussy, and the room filled with the scent of her arousal. Nadia accidently stroked her clit again and another tendril of desire shot through her. It was now clear to Amanda, there was nothing accidental about what was happening.

"You are a good little whore. You are almost ready for Master Alid," Nadia said as she dispensed with all pretense. Her fingers started rubbing up and down Amanda's soft labia. She drew her finger up, stroking once over the hooded tenderness of Amanda's clit. The touch wrenching a gasp from Amanda, her eyes flaring open before they settled on Nadia, who continued to chuckle.

"Stop calling me a whore," she groaned, her anger momentarily taking the edge off her desire and allowing her to focus on something besides the fire in her pussy. Nadia just laughed, and smiled devilishly.

The erotic torture continued, as Nadia used almost a dozen strips to take off every bit of hair. By the end, her pubic skin was puffy and swollen, almost as red as the now stripped away pubic hair had been. With the skin baby smooth, Amanda's pussy was painfully sensitive. She could feel the whisper of the air over her skin and her engorged clit.

"Nice and hairless. Now let us make sure your pussy is as sweet as the Master likes it." Nadia purred. She slid her slender index finger unceremoniously inside Amanda's wet tunnel. The penetration was enough to cause Amanda to squirm on the table, her hips rising of their own accord; her movement a silent plea for more penetration.

Nadia laughed. Looking her straight in the eyes, she brought the finger coated in Amanda's juices to her lips and licked it off.

"Not bad. But I think we can get you sweeter still, little slut," she muttered as she moved to get something from the shelf. Amanda felt tears of frustration spring to her eyes. There was no denying it. Her body was humming with desire. She must be some sort of sex-crazed slut. *Why else would I be feeling this way?*

Nadia picked up a small phallus shaped wooden tool. It looked like a honey dipper spoon except the tip had shallower grooves. She dipped it in the oil concoction, and once it was nicely coated she turn towards Amanda again.

Unable to control herself she could feel her pussy weep copious juices at the approach of the Harem Mistress. The exotic tortures gave Amada no respite; her nimble fingers spread her vagina lips and inserted the tool. Amanda gasped at the delicious intrusion.

Unable to control her responses she moaned with abandon as the tool was pumped, then twisted and turned in her pussy. She could feel her stomach muscles tighten, her pussy weeping copious juices. The delicious torture went on for what seemed like an eternity.

But as abruptly as the stimulation had started it stopped. Nadia stood back, an evil smirk on her lips. Her pink tongue whipped out and licked the honey dipper coated with Amanda's juices. "Yes, now you are ready," she whispered. "You taste very good," she stated in a hoarse voice before turning and leaving. The room was almost silent, only the soft sobbing gasps of

Amanda's breathing making any noise at all.

***

NADIA CLOSED THE treatment room door, leaning hard against it, her breath labored. The images of what she had just done, combined with the taste of Amanda, which still lingered on her tongue, had her panting hard. Unable to resist she closed her eyes and inserted her hand between her legs. The slippery wetness between her thighs made it almost impossible to get a good grip but she finally found her pleasure pearl and rhythmically started pinching it. She nearly sunk to the ground from the strength of her own orgasm.

Gasping she straightened her clothes. It would not do to be found in such a state in the harem halls. As she walked away she was satisfied she had prepared the girl sufficiently for the attention of their Master. Luckily enough Master Alid did not know that the assignment he had tasked her for was one she would undertake with relish.

After all, her secret preference had always been the fairer sex. Whistling she continued sashaying down the hall.

CHAPTER 5

"He'll take a lot of discipline, my sheikh," the trainer said, bowing low.

Sheikh Samir Ben-Alid considered the little man before him. He was of no consequence to him, so few people were. His family was one of the lucky few in Oman who had their hands truly in the oil industry. The nation, unlike their neighbors to the north in Saudi Arabia, had never developed a robust oil exporting business. Luckily for him, his father had possessed a great vision, bringing it to fruition first through the possession and domination of the port at Muscat, and then through carefully nurturing the Alid dynasty's oil empire.

It left him wealthy beyond most people's wildest imaginings, but it also left Samir bored and painfully unfulfilled. When he could purchase anything, what challenge was there to life anymore?

Sighing, he straightened the scarves on his head. To wish for the heat to abate was foolish. It was high summer and the heat would be soaring past one hundred and twenty degrees Fahrenheit today. All the more reason to be away from this dusty arena and back to his compound. At least pleasures for the tongue and of the flesh awaited him there, a way to while away the time and escape the heat.

Samir finally nodded at the horse's trainer. "I'd like a chance to inspect him myself."

"Yes sir, of course," the little man replied, bowing again and slinking toward the other stalls.

Bowing… they were always bowing. He was an Alid, and no one ever forgot their place. Not his underlings, and certainly not his lovers. Carefully, Samir reached out and ran a hand down the neck and shoulder of the Arabian. The stallion neighed and almost reared back, but Samir had been around horses his entire life. He didn't yield to the tantrum. Instead, he grabbed the horse's lead in his powerful hand and held it tightly, even as he stared the animal in its eyes.

Holding up his other hand, he commanded the stallion firmly. Samir did not shout. That would never do, it would just encourage it to bolt. No, this was a promise, a contract. He was master, and would lead and care for the horse if only the steed would honor and obey him. In all aspects of his life, whether it be taking on a servant, breaking a horse, or finding a new woman, it was always the same.

"Tornado, stop. You will quit panicking."

The horse stopped trying to rear and stayed firmly planted on all four feet. It shuffled a bit between its back and front legs, but did not attempt to rear again. Samir smiled and patted its neck with firm, strong strokes, letting his fingers ruffle through its mane. Within moments, the horse was gentle and calm.

"Very good, my steed. You know the correct tone at least. Breaking you, that shall truly be no challenge."

The horse nickered, a whistle of air hissing through its nostrils but did little else. Quickly, Samir made his way around the animal, cautious to give it proper warning and constant communication as he assessed its hocks and back hooves. Strong, well-muscled, and no visible injuries or defects that sycophantic little weasel clearly would have hidden.

"Very good."

The fact that it was the offspring of two champion lines, including a Tevis Cup winning grandfather and a World Equestrian Games champion mother was better still.

By the time Samir made a full circle around his newest acquisition, the insufferable horse trainer and his own assistant were entering back into the stall. "He has fine lines. Both of his parents are of pure Arabian blood, yes?"

"Yes, sir, only the finest of Arabian bloodlines and if you---"

"He'll do," Samir replied, nodding toward Yusef, his most trusted servant, both head of his security team and the only other man in his employ who stood close to his own six feet. "Give Farzod whatever he needs to finish the transaction, and make sure Tornado is delivered to my personal stables by the end of the week. I have a delivery at home to attend to."

As Samir walked back across the stables he mused to himself. It was just all too easy. A mere acquisition no longer presented a challenge to him. From childhood, he need only ask, and his father and mother would lavish him with anything his heart desired. As a child he had all the sweets he could eat, the best toys and games. As a teenager, he'd had a Ferrari by fifteen and an Aston Martin by sixteen. At thirty-five, he'd lost count of his garage and all the treasures therein.

If it wasn't for an internal steel, the desire to prove himself outside the pampered palace of his parents, he would have easily fallen into the decadent, corrupt life he had seen the few boys he could have ever called his peers fall into. Instead, he had devoted himself starting at the age of twelve to physical pursuits and the martial arts, as at least there he saw men who built themselves not through money, but through their own sweat. In wrestling, he found a pursuit in which poor men could become champions, and rich men humbled. He refused to be humbled, and soon his skill was on par with many of the best in the Middle East.

But, like the cars, like the horses, the challenge was gone for him. His life now seemed to be an endless cycle of ennui. It was enough to make him shudder as he pondered the future.

With women it was the same way. His harem currently boasted close to fifty members, and, in turn, he'd indulged in every desire a person could name. He'd had women of almost every nationality, every body shape, every hair or eye color. There was almost nothing left for him. Well, almost. There were some lines he had no interest in. Despite the practices of some of his "social peers," he never took a girl underage, and he never left any of his former bedmates destitute, nor did he physically force himself on them. He had no interest in truly scarring any of his lovers and concubines, not emotionally or physically. Sometimes they skirted lines, but that was the fun of it. Consent was always easy to get. For most of the women, they took one look at the opulence of his houses, his own handsome appearance, and they all practically fell to their knees to worship his cock.

It was what made it all so damned boring. When he had been a wrestler, the finest accomplishments came when he conquered an opponent who refused to just roll over, who fought back and provided him with a true battle. He wished for the same in a woman, a lover who wouldn't just spread her legs like a common whore at the sight of his body and his bank account. The challenge, the sweetest of victories, lay in a successful seduction.

He hoped he could have a challenge now.

***

BACK AT THE MAIN FLOOR of his estate, Samir oversaw a very special and particular delivery. The mattress was the best in the world, flown in yesterday as a special delivery from the maker in California. It was double quilted and could only be fitted with the deepest pocketed sheets. He already had the fine silk sheets set aside for it. He wanted it to complement his next bedmate. He'd only caught a glimpse of Amanda Cardwell this morning, a buxom redhead with an amazing ass he was already fantasizing about. It had taken an impossible amount of self-discipline to allow his number one concubine, Nadia, to move her into the harem quarters, and have her prepared in the beads and veils befitting a lover such as she would become.

When his men had brought her in, still unconscious, her body sprawled across the Persian rug with her hair framing her creamy complexion like a fiery halo, his first instinct was to turn her over and plow her like a brood mare, plundering her body until he spilled his seed into her. *That wouldn't give you the satisfaction of the seduction, nor of the victory over Hamilton.* The thought had helped stave off his lust, but just barely.

Watching Nadia barked orders to the assembled movers, clad in her colorful *dishdasha* that set her apart from so many of the common women clad in their plain black *abaya*, he knew that his plan would be successful. He would christen his bed and, with that, claim Amanda Cardwell as his own, until she never remembered the accursed Grant Hamilton again.

The culmination of today's events had started years ago, as the two young billionaires were still the young scions of their respective families. Traveling through similar social circles, their rivalry had been organic, both men having the combination of respect and personal pride that ensured a consistent game of one-upmanship regardless of the competition. Samir thought the matter had been settled when Grant had started dating his little sister Amirah, with high hopes of a marriage. The rival billionaire had broken his sister's heart, she now lived secluded with Samir's parents, her honor and that of the family forever besmirched. *And her virtue!* Samir's lips thinned with anger. *Vengeance is mine old boy.* Amanda Cardwell was now in his clutches and he had no intention of returning her intact.

He felt a slight twinge at forcing his people to play in the charade he had set up. Even his trusted Yusef and Nadia did not know the true depths of his plans.

The thought of his revenge and pending conquest quieted down the twinges his conscience sometimes gave him. Dr. Assad had informed him of Amanda's condition. It could not be clearer that this was destined to happen *Insha'Allah (*God willing*)*.

Yes, he wasn't only going to possess Hamilton's woman in every physical way possible; he was going to ensure that by the time she got her memories back she didn't want to leave. *The ultimate victory.*

He chuckled, as a thought crossed his mind. The Western cultures always said that revenge was a dish best served cold, but Samir knew better. It was best when scorching hot, and in the desert, it was very hot indeed.

CHAPTER 6

Samir looked on in anticipation as Nadia marched in with Amanda following behind her. Usually, Nadia made the blood flow fast and freely to his cock, with her sensual manner that spoke of her voracious sexual appetites, but now, even in the tight turquoise top and low slung silken dancing pants she wore, she did nothing for him. The American redhead? Now she was another matter. Amanda didn't walk with the same seductive sway that Nadia had, she walked like an American, very no-nonsense, focused only on getting from one location to another. Still, the violet silk of her harem robes clung to her in all the right ways. His cock swelled in his pants as he looked her over, and he turned away before either woman could notice his lack of control.

But it was Amanda's sharp green eyes staring back at him from behind her veil that intrigued him the most. Her eyes were so complex, simultaneously full of fear and disgust, but also…there was something there, a heat in the way she appraised him that had nothing to do with him being her nominal captor. Nadia had done well. His little fire cracker was still in the aftermath of arousal.

After patiently waiting and planning ever since Amirah's shame had been revealed, and his competitive rivalry had crystallized into hatred, he would finally exact his revenge.

"Nadia, take the guards and go," he ordered as soon as Amanda sat down to his right.

"Master Alid, I can always stay. This one has such a defiant mouth already."

"That's good," he replied, picking up Amanda's right hand and bringing it to his lips to kiss. She stilled beneath him, but allowed it, all the time her eyes trained on the scimitars his guard carried.

Samir knew the swords were a bit of grandiosity, but he loved affectation and his heritage. Besides, it definitely made the correct statement to people who considered crossing him.

"But Master—"

He narrowed his eyes at his head concubine. Nadia had been his favored pet for years, her enthusiasm for unusual carnal delights beyond satisfying, and her imagination matched only by his own. Still, she was forgetting her place. "I said leave us."

She bowed her head. "As you will, Master," she said, her hurt feelings scantly hidden. She and the guards hurried out of the dining room, leaving him and Amanda to themselves. Samir noted to himself that he would have to have a private discussion with Nadia later, to assure her she was still in his favor. She was not just a longtime lover, she was a trusted assistant, and regardless of the situation with Amanda Cardwell, he couldn't lose Nadia. Dismissing the issue from his mind, he turned to his conquest.

"Soon, I'll have my chef bring out some filet mignon. I thought something from your homeland might make some of this transition easier."

"Who are you?" she asked, chin defiantly held high.

"You do not remember me?" The thought of how easy her amnesia made his plan, had Samir smiling internally with satisfaction.

"I can't remember anything from the last six months and only bits and piece of anything prior to that. Your Dr. Ahmed says I have retrograde amnesia."

"Well, that is unfortunate. Nevertheless, that does not negate our agreement. I am Sheihk Samir Ben Alid and you are Amanda Granger. Your father's debts cleared and you as part of my harem for two years."

"I don't even remember my father. For all I know he is a first grade asshole and he sold me to this bondage."

"Or maybe you love him very much and will regret seeing him thrown into prison once you get your memory back? *Habibi*, let's not fight. Maybe you just need a reminder of how I make you feel?" Samir liked the chase, but a chase without reward was just frustration. He lived for a good hard fuck in a pussy as exquisite as hers had to be. While he was a patient man, patience was only a virtue for so long. He stood, even as his help entered and placed the steak and rice dishes on an oaken side table. Coming around to Amanda's side, he leaned down, and with his fingers unfastened the jeweled veil, wanting to see his future lover without the masking effects of the silk. His first thought was he needed to thank Dyana and Odella, their work was excellent. While they had started with a truly marvelous beauty before, the two girls had taken marvelous and elevated it to divine.

Her hair, a fiery auburn that matched his desires, was swept up into a bun with softly curled tendrils raining from it. Her coloring was set off by silver combs adorned with emeralds and white rose petals in her hair. She was a peerless beauty, a figure from a fairy tale, a goddess.

Leaning in further, Samir kissed the pulse point just below her right earlobe. "You, Amanda, are perfect. Has anyone ever told you that?"

***

Amanda almost panicked at his words. She felt herself shrink from the sheer magnetism of his watchful smile. After the "treatment" administered by Nadia she had come prepared for anything. However, from the moment she had laid eyes on Samir, she had known any number of women would willingly have thrown themselves at his feet for the opportunity to spend one night with him. He looked devilishly handsome, broad shoulders filling the expanse of his garb seductively. When her eyes had met his, she had frozen. He had unusual gray eyes, but what took her breath away was the desire blazing through them. Her clit was still shamefully sensitive from her recent orgasm; it wouldn't take a lot for him to convince her to surrender to him. She knew she was in big trouble. *Oh, stop staring at him before you make him want to rape you.*

The logical part of her mind concluded that he wouldn't have laid out this romantic feast if his intention was to take what he wanted. Clearly somehow he wanted the illusion of consent. Chiding herself that she even for a moment forgot this was *so not* a social event she set her chin in a stubborn line.

"I am no man's whore." Somehow it felt like she had said those words before, to another man, in another time. She glared up at him, her gaze challenging.

"*Habibi*, no sane man would ever mistake you for a whore," Samir whispered, one hand delicately caressing her breast through the thin fabric of her tunic. The breath left her lungs in one long rush as delicious tendrils of heat followed the path of his fingers.

Amanda bit her lower lip in an effort to stop herself from groaning. Her nipple pebbled under the wisp of silk.

"No… I," she started, but it was all she was able to get out. He nibbled on her ear lobe and pinched her right nipple oh-so-carefully, the pain and pleasure mingling deliciously making Amanda's breath quicken. Her arms drifted up, pulling him into her, unable to resist the inferno he was creating in her loins. *Oh my gosh.* Her body, already primed by Nadia, craved Samir's touch. *I need to remember.* She needed to remember. Remember what? Then it hit her. *We are in the Middle East. I'm in a harem. If I give myself this easily to this man, he is going to treat me like some unpaid whore for the rest of my stay.*

"Please, stop," she whimpered, as she leaned back from him, her neck exposed as his playground. Her pulse was beating erratically as he nipped and nibbled on her neck.

***

DESPITE HER VOCAL resistance to what Samir knew would be his inevitable victory, Amanda moaned, like a contented kitten. Samir knew he was going to need to sample Amanda soon or explode from need. He kept sucking at her neck, hoping to leave a mark, perhaps several. She was his now and everyone needed to know it. Her moans echoed across the room, and her nipples were engorged and rigid in his grasp. He lifted her easily from her chair, setting her on the table as he sought more, wanting to see her entire body under his gaze, open to him. Samir's desire flared, the sound of his newest conquest so close to completion.

Samir grew too greedy, moving too quickly as his desire flared high, costing him his self-control. He slipped his right hand down to the waistband of her pants, ignoring the way her hands clenched at his approach. Amanda stiffened again, but her moans increased in pitch the more he played with her areola underneath the silk with his left hand. "No...wait," Amanda begged placing her hands on his wrists.

"No, I think you're more than ready." Samir replied, forcing his hand underneath the waistband of her pants to find the smooth hairless expanse of her silken pussy lips.

She startled at his touch and pushed back, her feet coming up to push away at his legs. She was too shocked to keep her balance, instead becoming entangled in the tablecloth and tumbling to the floor, with a bang. Although clearly dazed, she frantically started crawling away on trembling hands.

The sight of her desperate attempt of flight was like cold water poured over Samir's flaming lust. Shame engulfed him. He was known for being an extremely patient and experienced lover, but somehow his renowned self-control in bed had flown out the window. Amanda Cardwell was proving to be more intoxicating than wine.

He knelt cautiously next to her, and pushed the stunning auburn locks back from her heart shaped face. Amanda's entrancing green eyes burned with fury back at him. "Amanda, forgive me."

"I said 'wait.' What was so hard about that, you arrogant aristocrat?"

"I thought---"

"Get away from me," she shouted, standing unsteadily. She weaved in front of him, almost falling, and he reached out, taking her in his arms to steady her. She fought for a moment, before collapsing against him.

"Then what did you mean to happen?" she hissed. There were tears swimming in her eyes, tangling on her long lashes, each one sending daggers into Samir's heart.

"I'm sorry, *habibi*. I should have exercised better control." He truly meant it. He abhorred men who were capable of harming women. Women were delicate creatures, made to be cherished and lavished.

"I just met you. My body might yearn for you, but I don't remember you. I won't let you possess my body before you possess my heart, never mind what I agreed to," Amanda stammered as fear started releasing its grip on her.

Samir was stunned. He hadn't meant to make her uncomfortable, not like that. He had never met a woman who had resisted him or wanted to resist him. *Such fire*. As his gazed trailed over her creamy skin and flaming hair he felt his cock hardening, even after what had just transpired. Embarrassed he shifted legs. *She was like flowing lava and a tornado combined.*

Yusef brought in the doctor, and Samir stood to leave, giving the doctor and Amanda privacy. “I meant to give you more pleasure than imagined. Forgive me.”

“No.” Amanda turned her gaze away, and the doctor implored Samir with his eyes to leave, lest her emotions cause her further harm.

In the hallway, Samir’s mind replayed the whole disastrous evening. Never in his entire life, starting at the age of thirteen, had a woman said ‘No’ as more than a token resistance in a sexual game, and never had a woman looked upon him with such fury. He was ashamed to realize he now wanted this woman more than ever. *Maybe even by any means necessary.*

Even as he denied the thoughts stirred by his mind, another part of him, the darker side that he rarely listened to, whispered something else though. He had seen, even as she was cursing him and gazing at him in fury, her hands drifting towards the marks on her throat and jaw line, where he had kissed her with so much passion. She caressed the marks, and the dark beast inside him knew she had enjoyed his touch, and it hungered for more.

CHAPTER 7

3 weeks later: Somewhere in the Middle East

"Grant, it's Alexander."

The satellite phone connection crackled, the result of a lightning storm causing local ionization. But Grant could tell it was his brother on the other end of the line.

"That lead we were chasing down just panned out. We finally know who took her. "

"Tell me."

"Sheikh Samir Ben Alid."As Grant listened to Alex report, the blood froze in his veins. Samir Ben Alid was a lover not a killer. But he was also ruthless and a vindictive son of a bitch. Unfortunately Grant knew he thought he had something to be vindictive about. However if he had hurt Amanda, Grant intended to pay him back in kind.

"Grant, are you still there?"

"Yes."

"Taking on the Ben Alid's is not going to be an easy task."

"Yes, I know."

"Tatianna and I will pull a rescue team together and will be there in the next forty-eight hours."

"Thanks Alex. I owe you one."

"No, you don't. What is family for?"

The line cut off, and Grant lay back on the bed. He was averaging three hours of sleep a night, and his body was exhausted. If he was to rescue Amanda, he had to be at his best, physically as well as mentally. He knew Alex, if he said forty-eight hours, his brother would be there in forty-seven hours and fifty-nine minutes, no more, no less. In the meantime, Grant needed to sleep, but he knew there was no sleep to be had. Instead, he pulled out his chair and started dismantling and cleaning his Glock 42.

***

"AMANDA, I'M SO GLAD you joined us," Samir said, standing and helping her with her seat before sending Yusef away.

"Us?"

Before Samir could answer, a young woman stepped through the dining hall doors. She was gorgeous, prettier by far than any of the other women in the harem, even Nadia, with dark brown hair that hung around her face in loose curls, and warm brown eyes that sparkled with a heady combination of warmth and seduction. Like the others she was thin with proportions that would leave most men on their knees, begging for attention. A woman like that would live in men's fantasies until their dying day, she was sure, and the merest whisper of her lips upon a man's flesh would melt his will to her every whim.

The young woman was dressed in Western fashion, jeans and a spaghetti-strap top, showing off the amazing hourglass figure of her body and highlighting her breasts, which were almost too perky to be believed. Sighing, Amanda covered her own curvier bust as best she could with her coral blue silk top. Amanda knew that only a couple of weeks ago she would have felt like nothing compared to this girl who really couldn't have been more than twenty. But she had grown quite a bit in the last few weeks. She had taken her rightful place as one of the women in the harem, and she knew the Sheikh desired her as much if not more than the other beauties. Maybe even more, as he hadn't slept with anyone in the harem ever since she arrived. She was currently the harem favorite. Despite knowing better she could not help being flattered. What woman wouldn't?

Samir surprised her by narrowing his eyes at the newcomer. "Jasmine, you can't wear that out later today."

The girl laughed and swept her long, dark locks back over her shoulders the back flowing down almost to her waist. "How many times must I tell you, Samir? I am not going to live by those ancient rules any more. You can thank your sending me to Paris for university for my lack of appreciation of traditional Islamic culture, but I find nothing wrong with my body. You can control others, but you also know I think it's your biggest fault." The young woman turned her gaze to Amanda, her mouth breaking open in a grin. "You're Amanda, right? He never shuts up about you."

Amanda blinked. This was certainly interesting. She had never seen anyone stand up to Samir before, and get away with it. "Oh, I...who are you?"

Jasmine leaned across the massive table so that she could shake her hand. "I'm his kid sister Jasmine, you know, the one he can't boss around and shouldn't worry about what I wear."

The tightness in Amanda's chest eased. "It's nice to meet you. But I must agree with your brother. If you wear that, well, it's like 120 degrees here. You're going to burn your skin to a crisp."

"Jasmine has to be appropriate in front of others. For the guards and for all other men, she has to have her body covered and she knows this," Samir said as if by rote, then his demeanor softened and he winked at his little sister. "However, I'll excuse your attire for now so when we see your surprise, you can be more comfortable."

"Thanks. You're the only brother I have who really gets me."

"I thought that was why you freeloaded," Samir joked.

The servant who came out this time was a small woman who continued to refill their coffee and also brought a platter of grilled lamb and various vegetables. Amanda's stomach growled and she dug in, relishing the tastes of turmeric that exploded on her tongue. While Samir had more than once provided her with what he called "American food," she had come to enjoy Middle Eastern cuisine as well.

"Big brother, I'm the most interesting guest you have," Jasmine replied, and then smiled genuinely back at Amanda. "Okay, second most. I like this one. She's got spunk."

"You're flattering Miss Granger because you want to go to America and will probably suggest she shoves you in her luggage for later."

"No, well, okay, but she's still more fun than the other girls. They just sip coffee and glare at me."

Amanda smiled, a bit taken aback by how forward she was. "I will sip the coffee, it's amazing. If I ever go home to America, you can come visit me. I don't think that'll be for a while. I need to get over this pesky memory loss first, but I bet you'd love New York or L.A."

"Oh Hollywood!" she said, standing and twirling about. "I could be a movie star anytime. That's my biggest goal!"

Samir shook his head. "Last week she wanted to be a doctor. Two weeks ago a dressage horse riding champion. She'll want to be a fighter pilot next week."

Jasmine nodded. "I intend to do everything that I can in life. It's really the only way to live. Isn't that right, Amanda?"

"I think so," she said, coughing and sipping more coffee. God, if this girl only knew the new experiences that Amanda had been having in her brother's harem. *Unless these experiences aren't new?*

"I can't agree more," Samir purred, grinning back at her and, damn it, her panties were wet again already. Samir had been a gentleman after that first messed up dinner, but in his eyes smoldered a desire and promise of pleasure that left her aroused almost constantly.

The trio ate their lunch with gusto, Amanda feeling comfortable as the diminutive Jasmine ate almost as much as she did. Samir wiped his lips with a napkin after his last skewer of lamb, and stood up. "So, Jasmine, would you like to see your surprise?"

She grinned. "Again? Father is right, you spoil me."

"Well it's more fun to spoil you than our brothers," he replied, standing. He offered Amanda a crooked elbow and she took it.

They walked arm and arm like that through the palace's labyrinthine corridors until reaching a gorgeous garden. It reminded her of the hanging gardens of Babylon she'd read about in history class. There was greenery everywhere, and even now, sprinklers were running to keep it lush. There were hydrangeas, lilacs, things that couldn't possibly grow here, but that must have needed a massive staff just to cultivate. The roses were exceptional, not just a deep blood red but also white and midnight purple. There were no thorns on any of them.

In the center of this garden was a beautiful Arabian stallion with a mane as dark as coal. He was held on a lead line by another female servant and Amanda grinned at his actions. However he'd done it, probably text message, maybe with just the power of his personality, Samir had kept his word so that his sister could be comfortable in clothing she preferred. She didn't have to cover up with only female servants around.

It was a sweet concession for his sister, and it made Amanda appreciate his heart and dedication all the more.

When Jasmine saw the horse she squealed and ran toward him. "He's amazing!"

From back by the rose bushes, Samir laughed. "Tornado isn't broken in completely yet. When I've finished taming him, he'll be yours. If you want to follow your passion for dressage, you should become the best. The only way to be the best is to ride the best. And with Tornado, you have a mount worthy of an Olympic champion."

She smiled at both of them and bowed low. "Thank you, brother." Jasmine wandered off with Tornado, the servant holding the stallion's lead, the young woman running her hands over his mane and neck.

CHAPTER 8

Amanda and Samir stood together, alone in the rose garden, her thoughts swirling. It had been weeks since the failed seduction attempt. Since then Samir had been extremely patient, happy to go at her pace.

She had to admit she could have never imagined sharing a man with other women, but in the last couple of weeks Samir had poured all his attention on her. His courtship was intoxicating. It had her toying with the idea of them together. *Emma would tell me to stop being delusional.*

The thought came unbidden to her mind, leaving her swirling in confusion. Who was Emma?

As Amanda tried to recapture the memory it flitted away. She took a deep breath and decided to focus on the now, instead of on a past that kept eluding her. Whatever feelings she had for Samir didn't change the fact that she was living in a gilded cage, and he was her prison master. But was she willing to give herself to him, knowing fully that he was likely to dump her for the next beauty as soon as she did? *The best case, I get a couple of months of his attention.*

Samir took a knife from his pocket and cut the biggest red rose for her. "Please, for you. It is not as gorgeous a color as your hair, but nature can only perfect such a shade once."

"Thanks," she said, taking the flower and sliding it behind her ear. "So what do you do all day here besides sex, buying gifts for your favorite sister, and amusing me?"

"I work a lot. My father and brothers make sure Alid Investments is profitable, while I work hard to ensure it helps others. We donate money to mainly orphanages and hospitals, people hurt by the wars that have torn apart the Middle East for decades."

"That's...wow."

He grinned and kissed her cheek. "You don't think that I can be both a hedonist and a philanthropist at the same time? That's a severe lack of vision, my dear Amanda. I am a man with many facets to my personality."

"You seem to be more than I realized," Amanda said, her voice dropping to almost a whisper level as she spoke her mind openly.

"How so?"

She swallowed her nervousness and started playing with a strand of hair, curling it repeatedly over her forefinger. "I'm just starting to understand that my impression of you was wrong. I think...I think there was a reason why I chose to come here, and that there can be something between us. Clearly, I have fabulous taste."

Samir smiled. In the last three weeks the worry that she

would regain her memory had been tormenting him. The lie that kept her docile and in his grasp had been uncomfortable to maintain initially. However the hotter his desire for her burned the easier lying had become. But Amanda intrigued him. Despite being in his possession, somewhere along the road it felt like she possessed him. He had rarely made so many concessions for any other woman.

He hadn't given up on his plan to get back at Hamilton, but it didn't seem as important anymore. He intended to master this woman, like he mastered all under his domain, but lately the willing submission he sought from her seemed less and less important. His need to possess Amanda was becoming an obsession. It was all he could do not to rip her clothes off and ravish her. Her weekly waxing sessions with Nadia were progressing nicely. Amanda's sexual inhibitions were being broken down step by delicious step.

"You do have good taste and I bet you taste even better. Don't judge me from any preconceptions you have about harems. I've had many women, but I have always been looking for the perfect one. The girls come of their own free will, and after they stay in luxury and have access to education and facilities they never could have dreamed of otherwise. Any who wish to go after their initial contract is up is free to. In fact, a few have."

"That's good."

"But I feel it's all practice for the one I truly seek."

Amanda looked down at the rose bushes, at the stems. Was it possible to have everything she wanted? The roses in the garden had no thorns, but could someone as amazing and handsome as

Samir have no drawbacks, no hidden strings?

"It all feels so fast," she said, unable to lift her eyes to him.

"Perhaps, but my desire for you burns like an inferno, I cannot wait forever, lest I blaze into nothingness." He looked at her with a feverish intensity. Amanda didn't know what to say. Her traitorous body was humming with need.

"I have a deal for you," Samir said, his voice laced with desire. As he continued to perpetrate the lie of her imprisonment he felt no remorse.

"I am not heartless. I understand that you have no memory of our arrangement. If you are not happy, I am prepared to set you free. I just ask one thing, Amanda."

"What?"

"I would like to spend a night of pleasure with you – see if I can't change your mind about leaving. That being said, I like unusual bed plays. I'm sure by now you can understand that."

"I should?" she riposted. "And what makes you think that?"

He laughed. "Feisty, exactly what I love about you. I won't hurt you, unless you want me to. But really I'm more into pleasure than pain. I just want one night with you to give you more pleasure than you ever imagined possible."

"Big claims," she said looking at him with uncertainty in her eyes.

"I can support them," he said, leaning down and kissing her, his tongue just barely touching her own in a tease. She moaned, her body pressing forward into his embrace. "Give me one night to have my way with you. You only have to say the safe word 'Jade' and I will stop." His grip tightened around her and he fastened his lips passionately against hers. His tongue slipped between her lips and danced around hers, in a sensual feast. When he pulled back she was breathing heavily.

"I want willingness. I might have been too excited at dinner a few weeks ago, but I always respect my bed partners."

"Really?" Amanda said, her breath coming in small gasps. She gulped and pulled back from him a little. "So one night? Anything I want and if it's too much, 'Jade' and I go home."

"You have my word," he said kissing her once more.

When Amanda broke away she was panting, nipples hard with desire. "I will think about it."

As Samir watched her walk away, he knew his conquest was almost complete.

CHAPTER 9

As she dressed for the evening, forgoing the normal hair accessories in favor of a simple flowing of her hair over her shoulder, Amanda wished she had more than five minutes alone to think.

Her body ached with the memory of Samir's touch. The more time she had spent with him, the more she knew that her body craved his touch. Amanda closed her eyes and moaned, her left hand reaching under the soft silk of her top for her breast. She shuddered as her nipple pebbled under her grasp, she was just about to slip inside her panties when she was interrupted by a sharp knock on the door.

Blushing, Amanda stood up and straightened everything, even washed her hands off in the sink for good measure.

A man, kissing her hands, sniffing the arousal left on them. The image drifted unbidden into her mind. Amanda stilled.

Who was that? It wasn't the first time this shadowy figure had emerged from her memories, but every time she tried to remember him clearly the image disappeared.

A part of her had been holding back from sleeping with Samir and somehow she knew the shadowy figure must have something to do with it. Not that she thought Samir was a liar, but what morals can a man have who forces a woman to uphold a deal which involves her providing her body as payment?

The sharp knock on the door persisted.

Any lingering arousal she had was snuffed out like a candle when she found Nadia outside waiting to take her back to the harem's wing.

"Great, what did I do to win the pleasure of your company?" Amanda snapped. This was the last person in the world she wanted to see right now.

Nadia's answering smirk made Amanda want to slap her; the other woman didn't have the right to look like she'd just won the lottery. "Samir wanted someone to give you extra attention on the way back, in case you stumbled. I volunteered."

"Like he believes you would help me."

Nadia shrugged and leaned in, her breath caressing Amanda's neck. "I have such things to show you, *little* girl. You need to learn your place," she whispered in her ear, causing Amanda to shudder in mixed revulsion and remembered desire. It didn't matter, she would never like Nadia, no matter how many orgasms the bitch in heat gave her. Moving back, Nadia glanced into the room on the left. "You wait there. I have one file to grab from Dr. Assad."

Amanda forced herself to smile. She knew that it was now or never. Her decision was made.

Regardless of how much Samir excited her, regardless of the

opulence and the luxury, she had to be free. No father worth his salt would sell his daughter in bondage to save himself. And if hers would, then he wasn't worth saving. She could not be another bird in this beautiful gilded cage, even if freedom was dangled before her as a prize. Freedom was priceless. She felt overwhelmed with sadness that he did not understand. The mere fact he had dangled it as a carrot in front of her meant she had to leave this place as soon as she could. *I wasn't raised to be a man's property.*

It wasn't that, at some level, she didn't want to explore more with Samir. God, the way she ached for him told her the opposite. Despite her body riding her hard in this place, which seemed to be built for decadent pleasure she wasn't completely stupid. She couldn't make a decision of such importance when she didn't know who she was. Who was the shadowy man in her memories? Somehow she knew it was important for her to remember, before it was too late.

It would take very little for her to fall completely for Samir, to even accept this lifestyle he offered, where she was one of many. Despite Nadia's sadistic games, it was because of her heart she was planning to run away. Samir's words and actions were as contradictory as her desire for him was self-evident. If she didn't get away soon, she would never leave. She couldn't give up her freedom, regardless of the pleasure. As remorse and loss at the thought of leaving Samir behind coursed through her veins, she turned and looked innocently at Nadia.

"How would I get anywhere? I'm too fat to make any real distance, isn't that right?"

"Typical overfed American," Nadia sneered and she turned.

It gave Amanda the opportunity she had been waiting for.

The second Nadia wasn't looking Amanda linked the fingers of her left and right hands together over her head and slammed her joined hands down hard on Nadia's skull. The woman collapsed to the floor with a thud, and Amanda was off, sprinting down the hallway.

She wasn't sure how long she had until Nadia woke up and ran for her. God, she wasn't even sure if Dr. Assad would figure it out and call for the guards with their choice of scary weapons. All she knew as she rushed down the halls and toward what she hoped was a main door between the wings was she needed to escape while the coast was clear.

As Amanda rounded the corner, she wished she had kept up with her exercise. Damn it, she was getting a cramp. Rushing through the halls, the marble beneath her was slick and her bare feet weren't finding stable purchase. As she hurried toward that large bejeweled door before the wide spiral staircase that she prayed hard to be the entry foyer, she slipped. Her legs shot out in front of her, and she went sliding, the silk of her pants reducing the friction to the point she looked like a baseball player going for a stolen base, as she slid directly into Samir, who was rounding the corner coming the other direction.

Breathing heavily, she got to her hands and knees and started babbling. "I can explain. I...Samir, Nadia's being a bitch … I .. I mean it's not what it looks like."

Beautiful and soft gray eyes looked into hers as lean strong arms picked her up. The ease with which he lifted her up made her mouth water. The sane part of her mind groaned disapprovingly.

Samir frowned back at her and stroked her hair back from her face. Despite herself, she leaned into the embrace. "I don't understand. Where's Yusef?"

"I---"

She wasn't able to finish as Nadia, flanked by the two large guards and Yusef, trotted up to them.

Samir dropped his hand from her face and turned toward the other woman. "What happened? Amanda says you threatened her."

"Hardly," Nadia barked. "The *sha*...American attacked me and tried to flee the compound."

"I didn't mean to attack her I was just trying to get away!" Amanda shouted before she could stop and think. As soon as she did, a deathly pallor fell over her face, and her hands clapped over her mouth. Silence fell and you could have heard a hairpin drop.

"Master Alid, one of the harem's cardinal rules is you shall do no harm to your sisters," Nadia said, looking up at Samir with eagerness in her eyes. "She's dangerous, Master Alid. She needs to be disciplined for her transgression."

Samir nodded his head and passed Amanda to Yusef's care. There was a spark of some unidentifiable emotion in his eyes. "We cannot have any woman in the harem attacking the others. This must be punished, but I am not sending Amanda away." His voice cold, his next words bore the steely tones of command. "Nadia, I expect you to undertake the necessary discipline. I don't want a mark on her however." Sighing, Samir kissed her forehead and walked away.

"Punishment?" Amanda repeated in a dazed voice. Could he

be serious? What had happened to her beautiful sheikh?

"You can't let her do this!" she shouted to Samir's retreating figure. It was at that precise moment Amanda realized she had nothing to bargain with.

Nadia looked at her with a smug smile. "Yes, Master," she said to Samir's back, before turning to Amanda and smiling with satisfaction, her voice dropping to where just the two of them could hear. "Don't worry, American. I promise to take really good care of you."

Two guards emerged on each side and started dragging Amanda away. "Samir! Samir! Please!!!!" As Amanda's screams echoed through the halls the sheikh was nowhere to be seen.

CHAPTER 10

Amanda found herself stark naked, strung up, her arms and legs each tied with black silk scarves to the posts of a four poster bed. Scared, she could only begin to imagine what her current position would mean for her punishment. The bed was luxurious, as soft a mattress as she'd ever felt, with rich yellow and orange fabric hanging from its posts. Around her there were pillows, rugs, and more candles than she could count. The wall to her right was almost floor to ceiling mirrors, starting just a few inches off the ground and continuing almost all the way to the ceiling. The air hung thick with the scents of frankincense and jasmine.

The opulence of her surroundings only increased Amanda's fear. If this luxurious room was supposed to be used for her punishment, what strange ideas did Samir have in mind?

The door to her left opened, and Yusef entered, wearing only loose black flowing pants, cinched and tied at the waist and the ankles with silken cords. She gulped. There was no way Samir would let Yusef touch her, would he? Relief washed over her momentarily as Yusef stepped to the side, crossing his arms over his powerful chest. Behind him however was Nadia, and Amanda felt a mixture of ire mingled with relief of the familiar. Yusef stood by the door, guarding the exit, while Nadia set her two boxes on the pillows below the bed. It was clear who the punisher was going to be.

"Why are you doing this?" Amanda spat out. "Where is Samir?"

"Where the Master is, is none of your business," Nadia replied, her voice was thick with danger and something else, something Amanda couldn't quite understand. She made quick work of setting everything else up, taking off her own top and pants until she stood there naked save for a translucent black thong. "In addition to punishment, this is also a lesson for you, girl. Today's lesson is all about pleasure and submission, the things you have to truly know if you ever hope of pleasing our master."

"I... where is he?"

"That's for us to know, not you," Nadia said, picking up a glass bottle of oil from the smaller box.

"Yusef, give her the tonic." Amanda watched helplessly as Yusef approached her. She knew it was pointless to fight him. Either she drank the liquid or they were going to force it down her throat. Seething with rage she forced her lips open and swallowed the concoction without protest.

Somewhere overhead, instrumental music, slow and seductive, with lots of rich woodwinds and soft tones began playing, making the whole room seem even more like a scene of seduction instead of punishment. The oil smelled heavily of nutmeg and warmed Amanda's skin almost as soon as Nadia's hands touched her skin. Her first touch was on Amanda's right shoulder, and Amanda stiffened. After weeks of Nadia's special treatment she knew there must be something else in those lotions, something aphrodisiac.

Nadia's skilled fingers worked their way over her shoulders and neck, kneading out the knots that stress had built there. Clamping her lips shut, Amanda couldn't deny the pleasure that was starting to radiate from her skin. She was used to Nadia's touch, and her traitorous body was associating whatever was to come with the forbidden pleasures Nadia had already delivered on her body. She blushed, but any shame was quickly forgotten as Nadia moved lower. Her hands, still covered with the aromatic oil, trailed over her breasts. For once in her life, Amanda was glad she was voluptuous, and could feel the other woman's hands as they lingered over her nipples and round curves. Nadia's talented hands tickled at first, just little touches. Unable to hold it back any longer, Amanda mewled and bucked her hips as best as she could, despite the constraints.

Even as her mind screamed no, her body betrayed her, and her mouth opened, a quiet sigh escaping. "You have probably guessed this from last time. The oils I am using are an ancient ointment used for the arousal of reluctant brides and harem girls." Nadia grinned. "Combined with the liquid you just drank, soon you will be begging to be fucked."

Nadia smirked at her and started twisting and teasing her nipples, working them up to full, erect arousal. Both stood peaked stiff, as the slim woman ran her tongue over Amanda's left nipple, using all of her skills to tease and taste the American's creamy skin. She started with tiny bites, the pressure measured just enough to entice but not hurt, causing Amanda to cry out in pleasure. Nadia pulled her head away far too quickly, but kept her left hand teasing her captive's nipple. The other hand continued its ministrations with the oil, trailing over her hips and then caressing her thighs.

"You," Nadia hissed, her voice deeper than usual, "are actually very beautiful, my *habibi*. It is too bad there is so much of you though."

Amanda's cheeks flamed. "Maybe if you had some nutrients in you, I wouldn't have kicked your ass. And don't call me *habibi*!" It was an endearment she only ever wanted to hear from Samir.

Where was Samir? Why would he leave her to this torture? Every breath felt laborious, every touch burned. Desire was flowing like molten lava through her veins, her every sense heightened and attuned to pleasure. Amanda started writhing in her bonds. Her body demanded delicious release and she knew she could not win this battle. Her inner muscles were tightening, aching for some sort of release. She couldn't… she needed…she, "Please make me come!" she groaned. Any embarrassment at the knowledge that Yusef was watching her being sexually punished was lost in the tidal wave of her need.

Nadia removed her hand, causing Amanda to whimper at the loss of her touch. "I thought you'd never ask."

The slim woman stepped out of sight, and for a minute Amanda thought that Yusef might step in. Amanda was so aroused she didn't care, she just needed her body filled. Her clit was throbbing, her juices running part way down her leg and her body sensitized like a thousand little jolts of electricity running all over her. Someone had to make her come and now.

"Yusef. The strap-on." The guard who had so far stood stoically reached within one of the boxes and withdrew a doublepronged dildo. The harness fitted like a pair of panties the only sign of its purpose a penis like protrusion on the inside attached to a bigger phallus protruding on the outside. Amanda watched as Yusef pulled the panties up along her legs. Nadia held on to his large bulging arms as she stepped into the strap-on. He pumped the end in and out of her until she was panting hard and her juices had properly lubricated the toy. The vision of him spreading Nadia's pussy fold to insert the dildo into her cleft had Amanda juicing even harder and wishing that was her.

As Nadia finally positioned the toy by inserting it fully in her own wet tunnel she turned to Yuself and said, "Thank you. You may leave us now." With no additional prompt Yusef walked out of the room. The only betrayal of his interest was the bulging erection in his pants.

Nadia turned with the harness strapped around her waist. She leaned in close to Amanda's ear, whispering words that Amanda knew were meant only for her. "As I told you before. You're going to be mine. Even before the Master, I'm going to be the one who your body yearns for. As I yearn for yours." Despite the fog of desire that had descended over her, Amanda finally understood. Nadia's desire for her was similar to Samir. This exotic woman wasn't a twenty-four hour bitch because she was mean, but to disguise the very real desire she had for women. Even as the realization dawned on her, Amanda knew she would not have cared whatever the reason was. Her body now craved satisfaction and she desperately needed Nadia and her strap-on to fuck her to blissful release.

Nadia positioned herself between Amanda's legs, the jutting blue cock sticking out from her groin. The molten avalanche of desire that coursed through her veins made Amanda yearn for her possession. She accepted the position, opening her thighs as much as her restraints would let her, her eyes beckoning. Desire now overshadowing any sense of embarrassment or shame. "Nadia. Fuck me, please," Amanda groaned.

The tortured words caused Nadia to pause her actions, her head tilted to the side. Nadia stalked across the room, untying one of Amanda's legs before throwing it in the air and over her shoulder, the position both spreading her open wider and hiding part of Nadia's face from the mirror's view. "Your desire is my pleasure, *habibi,*" she mouthed, as she lined up the vibrating dildo with the entrance to Amanda's pussy. "Know that as I fuck you until you scream in blissful release, our Master likely watches through the mirror with great enjoyment."

"Then we better give him a show that makes him regret he is not with us," Amanda said, her voice dripping with physical need. Her clit throbbed mercilessly and she knew she was ready to beg for it, on her knees if she could.

"Ask me again." Nadia replied, her lips that were hidden by Amanda's calf and foot, forming a smile even as she kept her eyes hard and unforgiving.

The stimulation of the dildo was so intense Amanda started to cry, she needed release. Sobbing she begged, "Please Nadia, I am sorry I hit you, please FUCK ME."

With a satisfied smile Nadia pushed forward, spreading open Amanda's tight walls, the vibrations causing Amanda to cry out in pleasure as her empty, aching body was filled. The dildos vibrations coursed through her body, causing her to buck her hips forward, trying to get more of it inside her. Nadia held herself there for at least a minute, keeping her on the edge, but not letting her get enough stimulation to actually come.

Amanda lost herself in the cascade of emotions, sobbing. "Please, Nadia. Please take me all the way. I'm begging you."

Nadia's hands reached around to hold Amanda's hips, pushing herself in fully. Amanda groaned.

"Yes, it pleases me," Nadia replied in a husky voice. Although the larger end of the dildo was in Amanda the other end was firmly wedged in her pussy, making her juices flow. "Now, you will feel it all." She started moving her hips back and forth, pumping the dildo in and out of Amanda's soaked tunnel.

With each forward thrust, the base of the strap on would nudge against her clit, causing the redhead to cry out in delight. Her nub was so swollen. She raised her own hips as best as she was able and fucked back against the strap-on with reckless abandon. The air was alive with the scent of the two women, incense, and spiced oil. The feeling of Nadia inside her, while her hidden hand surreptitiously stroked her inner thigh tenderly had every nerve ending in her body on fire. She stroked her fingers on her clit, pinching it gently, giving Amanda the last bit she needed. She came, her entire body quaking as she screamed, loud enough that the entire harem could have heard her.

Nadia pumped harder, relishing the fact she was both fucking Amanda and fucking herself at the same time. She orgasmed shortly after. She immediately took off her harness and dildo before cleaning herself up in a brief, businesslike fashion. Reaching below Amanda's line of sight, she drew out a pair of underwear, curiously cut into a boyshort configuration that to Amanda looked somehow thick or stiff. Pushing her legs together, Nadia worked the panties up and onto Amanda's hips. Amanda felt a round cylinder object inserted into her pussy. Looking her in the eyes, her face turned away from the mirror, she saw Nadia mouth "sorry" before pulling them on fully. She then turned and left without a backwards glance.

Amanda lay on the bed, exhausted and sexually satiated, wondering what Nadia meant with her apology. Then a soft humming sound started from the panties, the vibrations coursing through Amanda's clit, centering on the cylinder at the entrance of her tunnel, and she couldn't think at all.

CHAPTER 11

From behind his mirror, Samir watched everything unfold. He had instructed Nadia weeks ago to break down Amanda's sexual inhibitions. He should have guessed she would have chosen this particular punishment. His conscience was nagging him about the need to resort to tricks to get Amanda's consent. *I should stop this.*

He was reaching for the intercom button when Nadia pulled out the oils and his finger dropped away, traveling instead to the waistband of his pants, finding his belt. Alone in his viewing room, Samir opened his pants and grabbed his cock. Once he saw Nadia's hands on such round and willing flesh, he'd lost control, masturbating like he hadn't since he was a teenager.

He tried his best to keep a slow pace; to give himself the maximum pleasure he could from the erotic sight in front of him as his two favorite women shared pleasure. When Nadia stood up to put on the strap on, his eyes were slitted against the pressure building inside him, his breath coming in grunts and gasps. As Nadia's dildo had spread open the soft pink lips of Amanda's pussy, his hand sped up, pumping hard, fingers sliding over his sensitive head with lightning speed as the precum slickened his hand.

The still minute, as Nadia held herself inside Amanda, not moving, were torture for him. Especially as he saw Amanda's face flush, the pinkness spreading over her creamy skin almost all the way to her breasts, but he held back the pumping of his own hand until Nadia started her thrusts. His eyes closing as he imagined himself buried inside Amanda's long desired wetness, his cock spreading her open and causing her to cry out the way she was in the other room.

When Amanda came, screaming so loud he didn't even need the intercom to hear her wails, her fiery hair cascading over her face, he reached his limit, his cock spewing over the window and wall, soaking his hand and even his pants, leaving him gasping with his forehead pressed against the glass, trembling in exertion.

Part of him envied Nadia. He had wanted to explore the sensual depths of Amanda's body first, to be the first to spread her open in such a fashion and cause her to cry out so. He wondered if she would scream the same way for him. He didn't know, couldn't imagine such pleasures, but damn it if he wasn't going to find out.

As he walked out of the viewing room and straight to the pleasure room where Amanda was still bound only one thought was on his mind. He would be denied no longer.

***

THE SILK CLOTH WAS tight against Amanda's wrists. Sensitive

from her recent orgasm the vibrating panties were torture, her clit soon throbbing with renewed need. Did he enjoy what he saw? Was he pleased? All she wanted right now was for him to be please so he could release her from her heavenly torture. Her mind could barely focus, with the painful pleasure rippling from the panties on her clit, but thoughts kept swirling in her head.

Three weeks ago she would have denied it was possible she enjoyed what had just transpired, but in this world of heady desires she had finally discovered a side of herself she hadn't been aware off. The thought of Samir deriving pleasure from watching her sexual surrender had her juicing. She wanted him to have enjoyed what he had seen her and Nadia do. Never had she yearned so desperately to submit to another's sexual desires. Even as the words swirled in her mind she knew she sounded insane. As waves of painful desire continued to wash over her she fervently hoped he would come for her. In the aftermath she still ached. An ache she knew she needed Samir to soothe. She didn't know how much more stimulation she would be able to take before she burst into tears from the intensity of it all. As if materialized by her feverish mind, she heard the door open and he walked in. Tall, dark, and dangerous.

She licked her lips and felt heat flare in her pussy. He was delicious. Wild, untamed black hair flowing freely out of its confines and curling about his shoulders. He wore nothing now and she could appreciate the muscles of his abs, the dip in his hips where she could see the flesh curve around bone.

It was funny. She'd never really understood the point of calling something a happy trail, but she did now. The thin line of dark hair that teased down from his belly button to the black swath over his groin, only fueled her fantasies of kissing her way down it until she enveloped him with her mouth.

She swallowed at the thought. She didn't think she was that much into oral before, even in her fantasies about him since their deal. Now that she saw his erection springing free however, the girth of him and pink head, wet already with precum, Amanda wanted all of him. To please him with everything she had.

"I have not come to ask you for permission. I will not stop." His voice was thick with both promise and threat.

"I don't want you to!" she whispered back, desire making her voice husky. "I am yours, Samir, willingly. Please take me."

"As you wish," he replied. Reaching over, he picked up the remote for the vibrating pants and pressed a button, the speed increased so fast and dizzying that Amanda thought she'd pass out, the pleasure overwhelming her was so vast. Just when she thought she would pass out from overload he turned it off. With trembling hands he caressed her thighs and slowly pulled the vibrating panties off of her. They were soaking wet. Her clit was engorged and her vagina lips puffy. As he lightly caressed the entrance to her tunnel he whispered, "I wish I was the one to fuck you so hard your pussy got this deliciously swollen." Amanda moaned as every light caress sent bolts of electricity through her body. Her stomach tightened.

"This will not be over quickly," Samir warned with a voice thick with desire. "But you will enjoy every moment of it."

With no warning he spread her thighs apart, and thrust his cock hard inside her. She felt a jolt as he buried himself all the way to the hilt, pain only avoided because she had been so aroused for so long.

He was slightly curved, throbbing, stretching her pussy to the point she was crying in pleasure even before he started to pump. The curve of his cock rubbed against all the pleasurable points inside her, making the vibrating panties seem like a mild forgotten memory.

"For too long, I have yearned to bury myself deep inside you," he muttered through gritted teeth. Deep satisfaction colored his features. His cock throbbing inside her, Samir leaned forward and untied her arms. "I want you with me too." Amanda nodded, wrapped her arms around his neck, moving her hips as well as she could in time as he started to pump into her wet sheath in deep hard thrusts. His curved tool was plowing through her tender parts mercilessly. Again and again. Maybe the man wasn't human.

That had to be it, she was sure.

He was a devil, an incubus sent to tempt her and Amanda wanted him to. She was more than ready to surrender to the flame of desire that burned between them, regardless of the cost or outcome. Pleasure mingled with pain, and where one started and the other ended was impossible to say.

She was sure she had never felt this way before.

A shadowy image of a man in an Armani suit flittered through her mind.

Samir kissed her, tongue fierce and hungry, while one hand played skillfully with her nipple as his cock filled her again and again.

She was sure she had never known submission like this before.

A shadowy image of a man deliciously spanking her floated through her mind. Amanda stilled in confusion.

Samir pinned her down to the bed, lavishing her sensitive breast with his tongue. As he continued to pump her wet tunnel relentlessly full of cock, she was soon lost to anything but the delicious satisfaction of submission.

Amanda felt like her mind was being ripped in two, as fragments of memories overlaid with the pleasure of Samir inside her, echoing each other, the pleasure of each magnifying the other to the point she wasn't sure which was the memory and which was real.

Before she could recapture her memories the stimulation was too much. Amanda's thoughts were again obliterated as Samir thrust himself with intensity and passion. She screamed as he filled her again and again, pleasuring her body with his curved cock. She wanted to come, but still Samir had not let her, until she begged, her voice harsh with lust. "Please, make me come, Master Alid."

"Only after I come," Samir replied, his breath coming in short little grunts as he reached up and grasped her nipple with his fingers. He pinched the hard little nub just as his pelvis rubbed against her pussy, sending stars shooting through her vision. The clenching of her pussy around his cock triggered his release, and he bellowed, his thick seed filling her body with the pleasure and permission she had sought. She surrendered herself fully to the sensations, her own screams of climax harmonizing with his, until she collapsed on the bed, exhausted.

For long minutes Amanda lay stunned by what they had just done. She didn't think it was her imagination, although with the sensations running through her she couldn't be sure. But as he had pinched her nib, and she felt the first twitches of his orgasm in her pussy, he had grunted one simple phrase that echoed through her mind:

"I will never give you up."

EPILOGUE

Grant looked at the scattered pictures and felt bile rising in his throat. The evidence was irrefutable. Amanda with Sheikh Samir Ben Alid. Hand in hand, looking for all the world like a romantic couple in love.

The part of him that had sent men crying out of his boardroom was roaring in his ears.

She wouldn't, she hadn't. Not when he had been frantically scouring the world looking for her.

No, he would not believe she had left him of her own free will. This had to be a clever montage.

Whatever the truth he was going to wring the life out of Samir, very slowly.

Determined he turned towards the assault team assembled by his brother.

"Tatianna should have her by now. Get ready for the signal." He cocked his Glock and walked out of the makeshift tent.

PREVIEW BOOK (3): THE TYCOON'S REPLACEMENT BRIDE

Thank you so much for reading my book. I love writing and I hope you liked reading this story as much as I liked writing it.

If you are wondering what happened next, here is a preview of the final installment - *The Tycoon's Replacement Bride - Part 3.*

Montana Night

CHAPTER 1

Billionaire Tycoon Grant Hamilton, leaned forward against the barrel of his assault gun, and assessed the developing situation with narrow eyes. After scouring the world in search for his kidnapped fiancée, Amanda Cardwell, the moment had finally come to retrieve her from the clutches of her kidnapper. Based on information from Bahrain, Amanda was being held captive by Sheikh Samir Ben Alid, in the desert harem he was currently gazing at.

The Sheikh's secluded estate was built around an unbelievably beautiful oasis. It sprawled over an area extending further than 20 miles. The shade of the trees nearest the pool served as a resting place, created around stunning, lush gardens.

In terms of any real fortress like protection, it had none. Whilst the gardens and trees created seclusion and intimacy, they also obscured any view of approaching enemies.

Currently, a pair of six-man teams were scattered around the parameter awaiting Grant's orders. The men had been instructed to only shoot to kill if they absolutely had to. Hopefully, this rescue would never come to that.

More comfortable in the boardroom than on a mission that involved storming a guarded desert harem, Grant would not have been anywhere else than at the forefront of this assault. Snapping out of his musing he glanced up and noted the approaching dark, swirling clouds, moving steadily in their direction.

"I think luck is about to be our lady tonight."

"Really?" his brother Alexander replied, moving forward to get into a better position to cover the estate.

"Yes, it's another four hours until sundown, but with the overhanging clouds we will be able to execute the rescue plan in the next 20 minutes."

"I know you want to get to her as quickly as possible but I still think we need to give Tatianna more time inside the harem to locate her."

"We are going in as soon as the sky is overcast." Grant replied, his voice cold and uncompromising.

Alex took a deep breath. Although he worked for Uncle Sam as a spy and a sniper, he had relinquished control of the rescue operation from the onset to his brother. No one could argue with Grant when he had made his mind up. He was in his Louis VII mood as their mother called it. Still, he had to try.

"You are making this personal," he commented with a frown.

Grant continued to look at the dark mass emerging in the sky overhead, a dark storm to mirror the anger coursing through his veins. He remembered the blood on the note left for him. Emotions that had been bottled up since the kidnapping, started rising to the surface. Determined he stomped them down. He turned and looked at his brother.

"Samir Ben Alid made this personal when he abducted Amanda. I am not going to pretend. I want to wring the living daylights out of him, and pummel him to a pulp." His gaze reverted to the estate.

Alex sighed inwardly and thanked God he had better control of his emotions. "Be that as it may, this all seems a bit too easy," he replied. "I can't imagine that we've gotten this far and haven't set off any hidden alarms."

"What the hell are you trying to say?" Grant retorted, without removing his observation for one second, from the sprawling oasis estate.

"I don't know. I have a bad feeling," Alex replied, giving his brother a humorless smile.

Grant rubbed his temples, eyes still firmly fixed on the target. "I know what you mean. The trail from Bahrain that led us straight to Samir's door step seemed a bit too easy."

"Perhaps we should pull back, regroup, and negotiate Ben Alid's surrender," Alex suggested.

Grant shook his head. "It's not like you to be this apprehensive. I thought you were the big shot, super spy?"

"Well, I used to not give a damn," Alex said. "Now I've got a wife who at this very moment is infiltrating an enemy camp without me at her back."

"You are lucky Tati isn't here to hear you say any of this. She would kick your uptight behind."

"She would definitely try," Alex muttered and they both burst out laughing.

When Grant had met his new sister in-law, a couple of days earlier, a misplaced comment had her flipping him over on his ass. Tatianna Romanovsky Hamilton was an ex Russian Internal Security Agent. She looked like a curvaceous bombshell, but was deadly as hell. He was not about to underestimate her, or her skills again.

For two days, they had been waiting for the perfect opportunity for Tatianna to infiltrate the harem. When pictures had been taken of Samir and Amanda running around like two lovebirds Grant had almost ordered the men to storm the place. But the nerves of steel that served him well in the boardroom had ensured he stuck to the original plan.

It was well known in the area that Ben Alid was planning an opulent party and feast in the coming days. This meant a lot of unknown people walking into and out of the oasis estate. Despite the almost non-existing security, a stealth approach was the most prudent strategy. Tati had slipped in completely unnoticed, covered from head to toe, pretending to be part of the catering team. *Infiltration*, *extraction,* and hopefully *zero loss of life.*

Grant mulled over the risks of the operation as he looked through the scope of his AK47 rifle. Through the window of the east wing of the estate, a young woman was dancing. Her movements showed passion and joy. She was surrounded by other women, who were watching and clapping in encouragement. Yes, the risks were clear and present. If anything went horribly wrong not only Amanda, but also these innocent women might get hurt.

A tremor went through his body and for a split second, rage flowed, hot and pure, unmasked by his usual business veneer. Those who knew the Hamilton brothers always assumed that Grant was the calm, cool, collected one. Only Alex and Chase knew that sometimes, that veneer cracked, and the rage that poured out was lethal.

One day in middle school some older, rich punk had beaten up Chase and stolen his Sony Walkman. Grant had found Alex holding their younger, bloodied brother. Although he had no clear memory of what happened next, apparently he had made them take him to the boy, and given him such a bad beating it required three people to get him off of the poor student. The boy had ended up spending a week in the hospital and Grant had almost been thrown out of the boarding school. Luckily enough, Hamilton money had ensured that hadn't happened.

Ever since that day, Grant's emotions were always kept in check. He did not do anything on impulse. That was until he had set his eyes on Amanda Cardwell.

Although he didn't believe in love at first sight, now in retrospect he realized that was exactly what had happened. She had stolen his heart with one smile. The knowledge that he had put her in danger ate away at him, the demon of rage riding him hard.

Suddenly a figure emerged from the east corner of the grounds. It was Tatianna Hamilton, and she had Amanda in tow. They were making a run for it to the far end of the estate where the Sheikh kept his prized vehicles. Hot on their trail were men dressed in black from head to toe.

Men that did not belong to the harem's guard team, and shouldn't have been there at all. Somehow, something else was afoot, beside the covert rescue operation. Grant frowned. The men were gaining on the women.

He squeezed the trigger of his rifle and one of the men fell with a heavy thud. Even as Grant took the shot, Alex's gun went off simultaneously, and the second henchman fell.

Grant dropped his assault weapon, whipped out his pistol and started running. "I am going in," he shouted over his shoulder to his brother.

"I am right behind you," Alex responded grabbing his own handgun, and launched into a full sprint. *All units, stand firm, cover Grant and I,* he instructed over his handheld military radio.

As Grant ran, he knew he was being rash. Better men were at hand for this, but he zig zagged his way down to the estate anyway, trusting Alex and the team to keep the guards and any snipers off of him.

A gunshot rang out. A bullet whizzed past Grant's right shoulder chipping off the bark of a tree he had just veered past.

Heedless of the danger, he continued his sprint.

End of Preview

AUTHOR NOTE

Thank you so much for reading my book. I love writing and I hope you liked reading this story as much as I liked writing it.

As you probably know, many people look at the reviews on Amazon before they decide to purchase a book. If you liked the book, **could you please take a minute** to leave a review with your feedback?

You can do that at your local website if you purchased this title online.

60 seconds is all I'm asking for, and it would mean the world to me.

Thank you so much,

Montana Night

HIS PASSIONS WOULD NOT BE DENIED

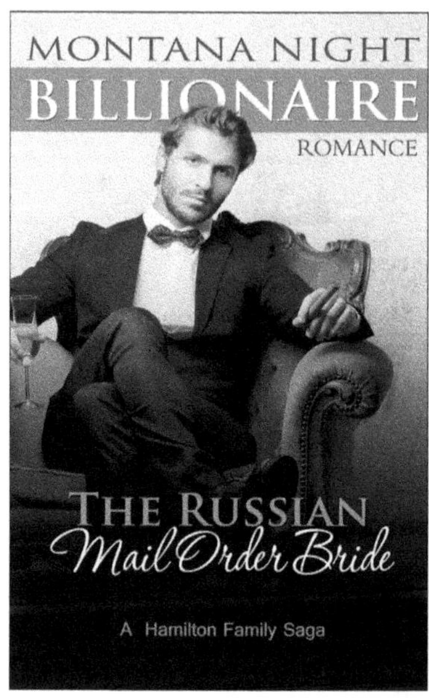

Billionaire Alexander Hamilton has hidden behind the persona of a dull, fop to deceive the world for so long he rarely shows his true self in public. But Tatianna Romanovsky might just be the girl to break down those walls. Ever since they locked heads, his legendary patience has been nowhere to be seen. When she is almost assassinated on US soil Alexander's protective, dominant, possessive male instincts flare to life, leaving him with an intense need to protect and claim this Russian mail-order bride.

Can be purchased at **amazon**, **barnes and noble**, **kobo**, **ibookstore** and other reputable online and offline retailers.

HIS DESIRE FOR HER BLAZED LIKE AN INFERNO

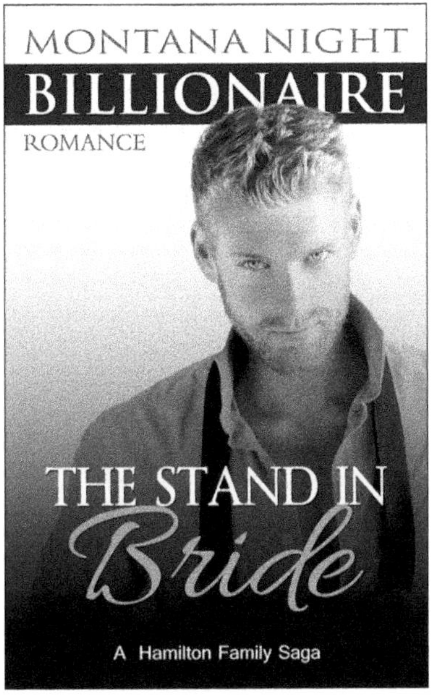

London born Rebecca Martin has spent the last four frustrating years working in the US at CorpSec a private security company catering for the rich and famous. Today, she just got her big break. An opportunity to be wealthy owner Chase Hamilton's personal assistant.

The man is lethal, has a smile to die for and the body and face of a very wicked angel. The attraction is instant, visceral. But she knows he's just too rich, too handsome, too everything to notice the way his plump mahogany replacement secretary has the hots for him. But a case of immigration issues with as Russian mail-order bride is just about to throw her in the path of her tantalising billionaire boss.

Can be purchased at **amazon**, **barnes and noble**, **kobo**, **ibookstore** and other reputable online and offline retailers.

www.ingramcontent.com/pod-product-compliance
Ingram Content Group UK Ltd.
Pitfield, Milton Keynes, MK11 3LW, UK
UKHW020135250726
13967UKWH00002B/674